Roscommon County Library

3 0001 00362778 5

uld h?

D0120878

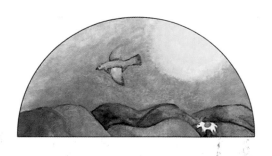

For Rodger, Jessica, Lissa and Lauren,
and Caroline, Libby and Tony Ardington - D.S.

For Niki, Jo and Leo, with love - J.D.

Text copyright © Dianne Stewart 1994
Illustrations copyright © Jude Daly 1994

First published in South Africa in 1994 by
Songololo Books, a division of David Philip Publishers (Pty) Ltd.

First published in Great Britain in 2005 by
Frances Lincoln Children's Books, 4 Torriano Mews,
Torriano Avenue, London NW5 2RZ

www.franceslincoln.com

Distributed in the USA by Publishers Group West

All rights reserved.
No part of this publication may be reproduced, stored in a retrieval system,
or transmitted, in any form, or by any means, electrical, mechanical, photocopying,
recording or otherwise without the prior written permission of the publisher
or a licence permitting restricted copying.
In the United Kingdom such licences are issued by the
Copyright Licensing Agency, 90 Tottenham Court Road, London W1P 9HE.

British Library Cataloguing in Publication Data available on request

ISBN 1-84507-022-4

Printed in Singapore

1 3 5 7 9 8 6 4 2

The Dove

Dianne Stewart
Illustrated by Jude Daly

Roscommon County Library Service

WITHDRAWN
FROM STOCK

FRANCES LINCOLN CHILDREN'S BOOKS

The great flood came to KwaZulu-Natal without warning. Thunder bellowed louder than a herd of bulls, and heavy rain clouds sent floodwaters racing through the Valley of a Thousand Hills. The flood took everything it could gather up in its arms – crops, animals, trees and parts of houses. But the house of Lindi and her grandmother stood firm.

COUNTY LIBRARY SERVICE ROSCOMMON

It was spring – planting time – but Grandmother Maloko could not plant her crops until the rain stopped. She spent many rainy days making beaded key-rings and necklaces to sell. But without her crops, life would be difficult.

At last the sun forced its way through
the cloudy sky. Lindi and her grandmother
hurried outside.

"Nothing is left," Grandmother Maloko sighed,
putting her arm around Lindi.

Just then a dove landed on the ground in
front of them.

"Look," said Grandmother Maloko. "It is like
the dove that Noah sent from the ark to see
if the floodwaters had gone down. Run, Lindi!
Get some food for it."

Lindi scattered the corn and watched the bird eat.
It was hungry. For three days the dove returned
to eat. Then it came no more.

When the land began to dry out,
Lindi journeyed with her grandmother
to Durban to sell the beadwork.
The station was far from their home,
and walking was difficult on the
muddy, uneven ground.

The train was full. A man offered Grandmother
Maloko a seat, and Lindi stood beside her.
Everyone was talking about the flood, the damage
it had caused, and the many lives, both human
and animal, that had been lost.

When the train arrived in Durban, Grandmother Maloko and Lindi walked through the tourist-filled streets. Between large apartment houses and hotels were small gift shops where Grandmother Maloko hoped to sell her work.

None of the shopkeepers bought her wares.

"We have too many beaded souvenirs already. You should try to sell them at the beachfront," they said.

At the beachfront Lindi helped Grandmother
Maloko spread out her work. People talked
about the difficult times. Lindi stood watching
holiday-makers enjoying the sea.

Time passed quickly, but by late afternoon
they had sold only one key-ring.

"Come, Lindi," said Grandmother Maloko.
"It is late now, and we must go home. Next time
we'll follow the advice of these friends and try
the Community Art Shop in town."

They walked slowly to the station.
Grandmother Maloko looked tired and worried.

Early the next morning Lindi looked out of
the window and thought about the dove.
It had been her friend and she missed it.
She turned to her grandmother. "Will you
help me make a dove?"

Grandmother Maloko smiled. "Yes, Lindi,
I will help."

They rummaged through the old tin trunk
for material – wire, pins, cotton and beads.

Grandmother Maloko turned on the radio,
and they sat down together at the table.
Lindi cut the material and her grandmother
threaded the needle.

"What has one eye and can change the
length of its tail?" asked Grandmother Maloko.

"That's one riddle I can guess," said Lindi.
"It's a needle!"

"You are right," Grandmother Maloko laughed.

First they stuffed the body of the dove, then
they worked on the legs and wings. Finally they
decorated the dove with beads.

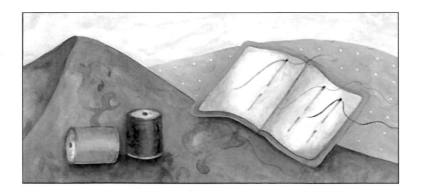

"Beautiful!" cried Lindi. "Thank you, thank you.
It is just like the dove that visited us."

Grandmother Maloko put the beads and scraps
away. "It is still too wet to plant the fields,"
she sighed. "Tomorrow you must return to school.

I shall go back to Durban to try and sell my
beadwork at the Community Art Shop."

"Could you show them our dove?" asked
Lindi eagerly.

Her grandmother smiled. "Yes, Lindi, I'll take it
with me."

Grandmother Maloko arrived at the Community
Art Shop hot and tired after the long journey.

"I'm sorry," said the saleslady. "We have too many
key-rings and necklaces already."

Grandmother Maloko shook her head sadly.
She turned to go, then suddenly she remembered
the dove.

She took it carefully out of her bag.
"How unusual," said the saleslady.
"It is beautiful. We have never seen
a beaded bird before. We'll take it."

Roscommon County Library Service

WITHDRAWN
FROM STOCK

Grandmother Maloko hurried back
to the station. Now there would be
money for food and fruit for Lindi
until the harvest.

Lindi was waiting for her grandmother. She ran
out to meet her. "Did they buy your beadwork?"
she asked.

"No, they did not," said Grandmother Maloko.

Lindi looked sad.

"But they bought your dove, and they have
asked us to make more."

Lindi jumped up and down. "I knew it," she said.
"I knew the dove was special for us."

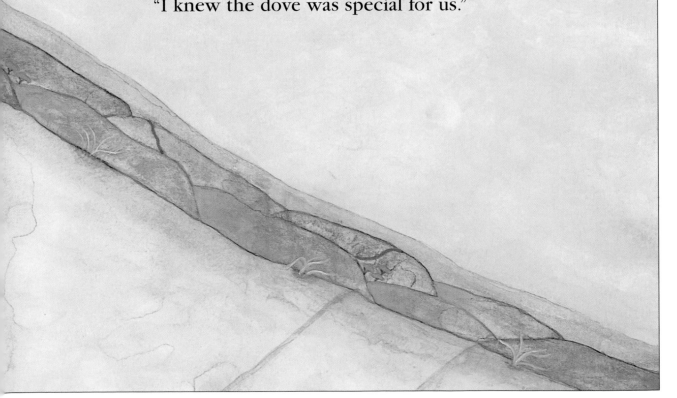

During that spring the earth came back to life. Grandmother Maloko and Lindi created many birds, people and animals from scraps, and the Community Art Shop bought them all.